NoraLee's Adv
on Planet Ifwee

Book 1

Written by Terry Nicholetti • Illustrated by Annie Campbell

GoldStar Magic!™

GoldStars and Thank You's to These Special People

Creative Team: I knew what I wanted GoldStarMagic™ and the Family Pen-Pal kit™ to look and sound like, but I could not make that happen by myself. So the Universe provided a very special group of people whose talents brought my vision to earth in a truly magical way. Annie Campbell—Illustrator—you gave colorful life to NoraLee and Loofi and their families. I didn't really know them until I saw them through your whimsical eyes and magical pencil. Patrise Henkel, Stafford Institute—Original Art Direction, Book and Kit Design Concepts—your ability to combine whimsy with practical design ideas translated my vision into a real product. Kristen Dill, Market Experts, Inc.—Book Cover Design, Book and Kit Design Execution—you joined us partway and whole-heartedly and skillfully brought us to the finished product. Jan Nigro, Song Writer, Leader of the Vitamin L Children's Chorus—Composer and Producer of *The Ifwee Song*, & Peggy Haine, Kaitlin Stilwell, Daniel Bonthius, Sam Harris, Bethan Lemley—singers—you gave us a delightful, energetic version of NoraLee's story. Cheryl Ostrom, second grade teacher—you wrote thoughtful questions to encourage family discussion. Michael Kincheloe, Karol Media—Kit Manufacture—you taught me how to pull all the kit pieces together—and then made it happen. Teri Gureckis, Dan Daniels Printing—Book Printing—you preserved the beauty and richness of Annie's drawings.

Friends and Allies: So many other dear ones provided ideas, support, and encouragement during the past two years. My sisters Joanne-Clare and Loraine Nicholetti, for unwavering support and generosity of resources, Janice Nigro, Director of Vitamin L for sharing expertise in producing music through a home-based business. Alex Orfinger, Publisher and Byron Adams, Marketing Director, The *Washington Business Journal*—if an artist has to have a day job, let it be as mine, a place where we get to use our talents, and where our heart projects are also encouraged and supported. (And Byron named the *Two-way Postal Card*™). Beth Zacharias and Lucy Webb, also from the *Business Journal* for generous text- and copy- editing. Jill Lawrence, Professional Editor and Organizer for editing ideas and inspiring the *Family Pen-Pal kit*™ name. Scott Stafford, Stafford Institute, and Nancy Benson, who continue to share marketing and management expertise. Kathleen Loehr, who told me to put the "big heart" in the story. Toy and Book Retailers Roberta Blanchard, *The Fairy Godmother*; Steve Shuman, *Trover Shop*; Carole Segal, *Treetop Toys*; Kate Karcher Clark, *Yattoy*; who all shared precious time and expertise. David Davis, Susan Hough and Jennifer Halls who helped me find Spirit and my mission in my art. My housemates Dena Huff and Jada the Cat for putting up with 3 a.m. writing sessions and overlooking my "household lapses" when I'm on deadlines. Betsy Crane, Laurie Kamp, Mahboob Asgar, Marguerite Beck-Rex, Deana Bodner, Annette Fuhr, Roger, Patrick, & Josette Garrison, John McGriff, Rev. Sylvia Sumter, my WISE friends (Women in South East—Audrey Thomas, Ruby Lewis, Joan Bell), Mary Ellen Kahn, Sara Lavner, Felicity Gage, for ongoing love and support, and for countless responses to calls and emails beginning, "Tell me what you think of this!"—And finally, Anthony Nigro, who at age 4, after hearing the first draft of NoraLee's story, said, "I don't get it," and after hearing the ninth, "I like it." I ask Spirit to bless all of you, and any other dear souls who in my effort to meet deadlines I may have overlooked.

Ordering Information for other GoldStar Magic™ products:

_____ Family Pen-Pal Kit (NoraLee's book, *The Ifwee Song* cassette, 6 Two-way Postal Cards™, gold stars, postal card sealers)—$19.95

_____ Family Pen-Pal Pack (same as kit, without the book)—$12.95

_____ Family Pen-Pall Refill (6 Two-way Postal Cards™, gold stars, postal card sealers)—$5.95

Terry Nicholetti
Gold Star Magic
611 Pennsylvania Ave SE #121
Washington, DC 20003
www.goldstarmagic.com
fax: 1-419-710-5518

Ordering information for Character building music by Jan Nigro and the Vitamin L Children's Chorus:

Vitamin L
105 King St.
Ithaca, NY 14850
E-mail: vitaminLproject@hotmail.com

NoraLee's Adventures on Planet Ifwee

Copyright 2001 by Terry Nicholetti

ISBN 0-9716488-0-8

Library of Congress Control Number: 2001098938

Printed in the United States of America

I dedicate this book with love to my mother Antoinette and
my father Felix who shaped my past,
to my daughter Kathy who helped create my present,
to my granddaughters Keela, Chantelle,
and Olivia and their friends Jocelyn, Gabby, and Natalie,
who inspire my hope for the future, and
to Doctor Connie Hendrickson, who, in
Spring of 2000, first said to me,
"Good job, Terry; give yourself a gold star!".

NoraLee Johnson was climbing her tree
  When she heard Mama calling, "Come here, NoraLee!"

So she sat very still on her favorite bough,
  As her Mama got louder, "YOU GET HERE RIGHT NOW!"

"Oh, I know I should answer," she thought, "but how come—
  Just to clean up my room, or do something else dumb?"

NoraLee thought of Toby,
    her own little brother.
He NEVER got called on
    to help out their mother.

Besides, she was feeling a bit sad today;
    "I wish Grandma and Grampa had not moved away."

NoraLee wondered how long it would be
    'Til her mama would notice her up in the tree.

Then she blinked — what was THAT? — flying right past her porch—
    A bright golden ball with a tail like a torch!

The ball landed softly. It shook and it wiggled.
　　A strange little boy tumbled out with a giggle.
He smiled, his voice crackled, "What's up, NoraLee?
　　I am Loofi Mondel from the Planet Ifwee.

We're about a bazillion-and-one miles away,
　　And I've traveled the heavens to come here to play.
But just as my space ship was ready to land
　　I could hear you say something I don't understand."

"Oh yeah?" NoraLee said, her voice a bit gruff,
   So this strange little creature would know she was tough.

"Oh, yeah," Loofi said, "I heard grumbling and sighing
   About helping out, which is so satisfying!"

"You're weird," NoraLee said. "I just don't like cleaning."
"Why not?" Loofi asked her. "I don't get your meaning.

On Ifwee, we always feel proud and have fun,
By deciding and doing what needs to be done!"

NoraLee was so puzzled by what Loofi said
    That she scrunched up her eyes and was scratching her head.

Then she noticed a tingle was tickling her toes.
    And it slithered inside her and niggled her nose.
    When it fluttered her eyelids and shivered her chin,
        She could feel an adventure about to begin.

So she thought for a minute, then feeling courageous,
   Said, "Loofi, I think what you're saying's outrageous.
But maybe – if there was a way I could see...."
   "All right!" Loofi cried, "Come to Ifwee with me!"

"Well, ok," NoraLee said, "but let's make it snappy.
   If I miss my dinner my mom won't be happy."
"No problem," said Loofi, "I'm faster than light.
   Now let's get to my ship and get ready for flight."

Loofi revved up the engine as they took their seats,
    Pushing buttons that blinked, making strange blips and bleeps.

NoraLee's heart was pounding; could they really fly?
    Oh, she'd be very brave – or at least she would try.

Then before she could whistle three notes of a tune,
  They were soaring through clouds, zooming right by the moon.

Passing millions and billions and trillions of stars,
Passing planets like Pluto and Saturn and Mars.

In a split-second flash they touched down with a bump.
"Hey it's Ifwee! We've landed! Come on now, let's jump!"

NoraLee Johnson was not at all scared.
But she kept her eyes open so she'd be prepared,
In case oogely boogelies might want to eat her,
Or giant computers might try to delete her!

But soon she could tell everything would be fine,
When she looked up and saw Ifwee's welcoming sign.

Welcome to

IfWee

Population 3,261

If we care, it's magic-

GOLD STAR

MAGIC

Loofi was grinning. He said, "NoraLee,
This is the magic on Planet Ifwee.
It's why we don't mind when we're doing our chores.
We just do what we care about—not a thing more!"

"I don't get it," said NoraLee,
"what are you saying?"
You care about cleaning
when you could be playing?"

Loofi laughed, "We don't care about cleaning up stuff.
We just care about keeping our homes nice enough.
We don't tell you to love everything you must do.
We just ask you to know why it matters to you."

"Why it matters to me? I don't get what you mean.
      It's my Mama who tells me when I have to clean."

"Well, of course," Loofi answered, "when you were a baby,
      The grownups decided each 'yes, no and maybe.'
But we're growing up now. So we get to see
      How to choose what's important to you and to me.

Now just tell me the chores that you don't like to do.
      And then come meet some folks with a different view."
NoraLee gave some thought; then she said, "I suppose
      That I really don't like washing up dirty clothes."

"So come meet Robinia Clarinda Gazaundry!
   She's helping her dad with the family laundry."

"Hello, NoraLee. I know just what you mean.
   I used to not care if my clothes weren't clean.

But did you ever notice how you can feel grumpy,
   When things that you're wearing are wrinkled and frumpy?"

"So now we make time to take care of our clothes,
And we feel very proud from our hats to our toes!"

NoraLee wasn't sure she could WANT to do laundry.
But still she said "thanks" to Robinia Gazaundry.

Then Loofi said, "Tell me,
  what *else* makes you stress?"
NoraLee said, "When Mama yells,
  'Your room's a mess!'"

"Sounds like time to meet
  Mather and Dunobbi Shroom.
Let's *see* how they feel about
  cleaning *their* room."

"Howdy do," Mather said. "Here's the truth about us—
  There are times when we don't even care about dust.

  But did you ever notice you'll grumble and mutter
    When your favorite playthings are lost in the clutter?

"So that's a good reason to put things away –
      To be sure we can find them the next time we play!

And whenever there's something that's got to be done,
      Try to do it together — it's so much more fun!"

"Thanks," said NoraLee. "But is anyone able
      To have any fun when they're clearing the table?"

Loofi said, "Meet my Grandmother Grayleah Thrishes.
        She helped me make sense out of doing the dishes!"

"Good day, NoraLee. What a pleasure to meet you!
        I know dirty dishes can sometimes defeat you.
But can you imagine them piled to the ceiling?
        If we never washed them, we'd surely be feeling
A little bit sick when they started to stink.
        And on what would we eat? Tell me, what do you think?"

NoraLee smiled
    as she pictured the scene.
"Yes I think I'm beginning to get
    what you mean.

If a grownup in charge gives you something to do,
    Like some chore that can seem really boring to you,

Ask, 'Why do I care?' Take some time to think through it.
    If we care, it's magic, and that's why we'll do it!"

Everyone cheered, "Way to go, NoraLee!
    You'll be helping yourself and your whole family!"

"Be proud," Loofi said, "of the person you are.
    Every time you help out, give yourself a gold star!"

"And then," said Robinia, "here's what you do.
　　Tell your Grandma, or somebody else who loves you."

"That's right, " said Dunobbi, "whenever you share
　　A proud moment with somebody special who cares,

The whole family gets GoldStar Magic!

NoraLee sighed, "Grandma and Grandpa would care.
　　But they've just moved away - I'm not even sure where."
"Don't you worry," said Loofi. "It's not really tragic.
　　'I know just the way to share *your* Gold Star Magic.

This card is for you and your Mama to write
　　Something special you're proud of; then mail it tonight.
I am sure, when your Grandma and Grampa receive it,
　　They'll be so delighted—Oh, you can believe it—
The very next thing they'll decide they must do
　　Is to write their encouraging words back to you!"

"Hey, we'll be family pen-pals!" cried out NoraLee.
   "I can't wait 'til they send their first answer to me!"

Grandma Grayleah nodded, "You're going to be great!"
   Yes!" agreed NoraLee, "And I'm going to be late!"

Loofi smiled. "We can hurry; let's get in my ship.
   And whenever you want, we can take a new trip."

29

So before they could whistle three notes of a tune,
 They were soaring through clouds, zooming right past the moon.

In a split-second flash they touched down with a bump.
 "Hey, we've landed! Bye, Loofi! I'm ready to jump!"

NoraLee waved goodbye to the vanishing ball,
  And she started towards home as she heard Mama call,

"Where's that NoraLee Johnson? I need you right now!"
  OK, Mama, I'll help you, if you tell me how!

Feeling proud, NoraLee saw her Mama's surprise.
    And she felt kind of warm from the love in her eyes.
Mama said, "Where on earth did you get that cool card?"
    "Not on earth," NoraLee answered, hugging her hard.

At the same time, a tingle was tickling her toes,
    And it slithered inside her and niggled her nose.

Then it fluttered her eyelids, and—here's the best part—
    She could feel GoldStar Magic just filling her heart.